the MONSTER
at the end of this book

By Jon Stone
Illustrated by Michael Smollin

A GOLDEN BOOK • NEW YORK

Visit us on the Web!
www.randomhouse.com/kids

Educators and librarians, for a variety of teaching tools, visit us at www.randomhouse.com/teachers

Library of Congress Control Number: 2003107954
ISBN: 978-0-375-82913-0 (trade)—ISBN: 978-0-375-92913-7 (lib. bdg.)
PRINTED IN MALAYSIA
14 13 12 11 10 9 8

Listen, I have an idea. If you do not turn **any pages**, we will never get to the end of this book.

And that is good, because there is a **Monster** at the end of this book.

So please do not turn the page.

Maybe you do not understand. You see, turning pages will bring us to the end of this book, and there is a **Monster** at the end of this book...

...but **this** will stop you from turning pages. See? I am tying the pages together so you cannot....

THERE! I, Grover, am nailing this page to the next one so that you will not be able to turn it, and we will not get any closer to the Monster at the end of this book.

ALL RIGHT!! ALL RIGHT!! ALL RIGHT!!

Do you know that every time
you turn another page . . .
you not only get us closer
to the MONSTER at the end
of this book, but you make
a terrible mess.!

The next page is the end of this book, and there is a **MONSTER** at the end of this book.

Oh, I am so **SCARED!**

Well, look at that! This is the end of the book, and the only one here is ...

ME

I, lovable, furry old **GROVER,** am the Monster at the end of this book.

And <u>you</u> were so **SCARED !**

THE
END

I told you
and told you
there was
nothing to be
afraid of.